A Walk with Sarah

A Walk with Sarah

Patricia Rogers Bisgrove

Patricia Rogers Bisgrove

Library of Congress Control Number: 2009902430
ISBN: Hardcover   978-1-4415-1969-6
                   Softcover   978-1-4415-1968-9

This book was printed in the United States of America.

To order additional copies of this book, contact:
Xlibris Corporation
1-888-795-4274
www.Xlibris.com
Orders@Xlibris.com
60125

Dedication:

Grand Master Jon Loren, who inspired me to write this book.

My Thanks:

To my writing group: Cheri, Gina, Kidd, and Maureen.

Chapter 1

Sarah Clarke ran out of the classroom as soon as the three o'clock bell rang. She didn't even wait for Mrs. Dominick to dismiss the class. Sarah headed down the hall, clutching her books close to her chest, while her book bag swung by her side. Tears began to stream down her freckled face. Her white cotton blouse hung outside the skirt of her blue and white plaid uniform. Sarah's dirt speckled socks had slipped down to the rim of her scuffed shoes, making her look like a street urchin. She finally made it to the big wooden doors that led to the outside of the school, pushing them wide open as she ran through, then hurried down the front steps to her bus. Her bus was always the first one to leave the school grounds, and today Sarah was glad it did.

Sarah greeted Hal, the bus driver, then went to the rear of the bus and sat in the far corner of the back seat. As she began to put her books into her book bag, Sarah exclaimed, "Oh no!" In her rush, she had forgotten her lunch box. Now she would have to tell her mother why. That would be a problem.

Sarah's mom was a wonderful woman, but she always thought the teachers knew best. It would be Sarah's fault if something went wrong. There were never any harsh words, only the words that Sarah knew by heart: *You must try harder, dear; the teacher just wants to bring out the best in you.*

Sarah did try hard and studied late into the night, but it never did any good. She couldn't write down the right answers to the test the next day. She knew the answers, but the questions weren't worded right, so she would fail the test and have to stay in at recess.

Like today, Mrs. Dominick had asked Georgia to read off the spelling words, as Sarah wrote them on the blackboard. Georgia sat in the front row, while Sarah stood facing the blackboard, with the white chalk in her hand, and wrote the spelling words on the board as they were called out.

When they were finished, Georgia smiled and said, "Let's go outside now." Georgia ran to tell Mrs. Dominick that the spelling test was on the board and that she and Sarah were going to play. The bell rang in ten minutes, and all the classes lined up in front of the school steps where their teachers were standing.

At the back of the line, Georgia said, "Wait till I tell you what Sarah did. She wrote the spelling words on the blackboard and they were all wrong. She isn't too smart."

Sarah could hear them say her name and laugh. All Sarah could think of was the spelling words on the front blackboard. Mrs. Dominick was always the first one in the room, and as usual, she was standing on the platform that held her desk, chair, and a podium for her books.

Mrs. Dominick said, "Sarah, stand by your desk and then we'll go over your spelling words." Sarah stood up, looking at no one but the teacher.

Then it began. Mrs. Dominick pointed to the first word and asked, "Could anyone spell 'desert' correctly?"

Georgia raised her hand, stood up and spelled desert. Then she smiled at everyone and sat down. There were twenty-five words on the board, and Sarah knew they were all wrong. How could she stand there and listen to the class spell them correctly? But she did.

Mrs. Dominic said, "Sarah, you will write them twenty-five times each by tomorrow." Sarah sat down, not looking at anyone, and stared at the desktop in front of her.

Georgia whispered to Mary Jane, "Everyone knows desert has only one "s" not two."

Mary Jane said, "Maybe she thought about a dessert she likes, instead of being out in a desert."

Chapter 2

Sarah sat on the bus and didn't hear anyone else get on. All she kept thinking was, *Why am I so dumb? I study and I try. What is wrong with me?* Peter sat down next to her and began to talk, but Sarah didn't hear a word Peter said. She just kept looking out the window. When her stop came, she got up and walked down the aisle, listening to everyone talking about what they were going to do when they got home.

She waved goodbye to Hal and climbed down the bus steps. She walked to the bench located in the small park in front of a few stores, where she always waited for her mother to pick her up. Suddenly it began to rain, and Sarah ran toward one of the stores that had an overhang jutting out. As she ran through the parking lot, she stepped in the only small puddle in the whole parking lot. *Of course*, thought Sarah, *a 'perfect' end to my rotten day.* Now she had muddy shoes and socks, instead of just dirty ones.

She stood there for a few moments, watching the rain, when she heard music coming from behind her. She turned around and looked through the large bay window in front of her. On the large sign over the big black door were the words *Club Center International Northern Tai Chi Gung-Fu Association.* She wondered what that meant. She could see people inside, both young and old, moving very slowly to music. This fascinated her; she cupped her hands to the sides of her face and pressed her nose against the glass. Now she could see clearly what was going on inside the room.

The students had on black uniforms with red trim around the edges of the jackets and black shoes on their feet. She had never seen shoes like that and wondered why they didn't wear tennis shoes. Sarah saw a big clock on the wall in the back of the room; it was four thirty. *Mom is really late this time; maybe she had to finish up some work that Mr. Thomas wanted done at the last minute.* Sarah turned and looked around the parking lot to see if her mother had driven up while she was looking in the window, but she hadn't. When Sarah turned around again, she was facing a tall man dressed in black, smiling at her through the window. Sarah jumped back and then laughed.

"Come inside," the man said, but she shook her head *no.*

"Sarah," her mother called. Sarah turned and ran to her mother's car jumping over some of the puddles of water.

Chapter 3

On the way home, she told her mother about the people in the building and that they were moving slowly to music. "I would like to try to do that."

Her mother smiled and said, "They are in a *Tai Chi* class run by Sifu Jon." As they drove home, the conversation changed.

Sarah's mother asked, "How was school today?"

Sarah thought to herself, *Do I just tell her about the test or 'everything' about the test?* Sarah looked out of the car window and said, "I failed my spelling test."

Her mother looked over at her and said, "How could that be? You knew all the words when we went over them last night." Sarah just looked ahead and shrugged her shoulders.

Sarah and her mother talked about other things while they made dinner. Then they sat down at the table. Sarah's mother said, "I have a surprise to tell you."

Sarah asked, "What is it?"

"I have a new job at the office. Mrs. Johnson is leaving town and Mr. Thomas asked me if I would like the job."

Sarah was so happy; she jumped up and hugged her mother and asked, "What did you say?"

"Of course I said yes. The only problem with this job is, I'll be working longer hours now. So we have to find a place for you to stay until I am able to pick you up at five."

Sarah couldn't get the words out of her mouth fast enough. "What about the *Tai Chi* place? I could take lessons and be safe at the same time."

Her mother paused, and then said, "I'll think about it and give you an answer in the morning." After dinner, Sarah helped with the dishes and then went to her room to do her homework.

Her mother walked to the hallway and picked up the telephone directory, looked up two numbers, and made two calls. When she finished making the first call, she smiled and hung up the phone. Then she called Mrs. Rogers, who lived two houses down from them. Mrs. Rogers took care of two other young girls after school.

Mrs. Clark asked, "Would it be possible for Sarah to stay with you in the afternoon too?"

Mrs. Rogers said that Sarah could stay three days a week at her home.

Sarah heard her mother's call the next morning to get out of bed and get ready for school. Sarah came down the hall, tucking her blouse into the back of her uniform. She sat down and began to eat her Cheerios while thinking, *How can I bring up the Tai Chi school?*

Her mother's voice broke into her thoughts: "I made two calls last night. The first one was to Sifu Jon about you taking a class, and the second one was to Mrs. Rogers about you staying with her three days a week." Sarah nearly choked on her cereal.

Sitting there looking at her mother, she asked, "What did Sifu say?"

Her mother told her that she would be able to join the class today. "You'll be at the *Tum Pai Tai Chi* School two days a week, and three days with Mrs. Rogers."

Chapter 4

Sarah was on cloud nine the whole day and couldn't wait to go to her afternoon class. When Hal pulled up to the colorful little building, she nearly ran off the bus. As she entered the classroom, she noticed the *Tai Chi* students bowing before they entered the room. She stood there not knowing what to do, when she heard a voice behind her say, "Welcome."

Sarah turned. It was the same man who had been at the window yesterday. He told her his name was Sifu.

"Mine is Sarah," she replied.

Sifu spoke, "Your mother called to enroll you in beginner's *Tai Chi*. Let me show you how to bow before entering the classroom. First, you make a fist with your right hand, and then cover that hand with the palm of your left hand. Then holding your hands in that position, you bring them towards you stomach and bow from the waist."

Sarah did this, and then Sifu told her to sit on the bench, where he would tell her about the lineage of the school and about internal energy *(Chi)*, and how it flows through the body.

Sarah told Sifu that she thought it sounded weird about *Chi* in her body.

Sifu said, "Everyone has *Chi*, but you must learn how to use it." He continued to explain about how the breath, movement, and *Chi* are all hooked together.

This information was very interesting, but Sarah couldn't wait to begin learning *Tai Chi*. Sifu said, "Some people start and do not last, while others continue to work and learn." He also explained that *Tai Chi* was something she would not learn overnight. "It takes practice, and you must not be in

13

a hurry to move on to the next step before you are ready." He said, "I'll tell you when you are ready. Sometimes there will be setbacks, but you should remember practicing will only help you to improve. *Tai Chi* is the highest form of the martial arts. It is also an art that never stops teaching you something new."

Sifu told her the first thing she would learn would be how to walk.

Sarah asked, "Walk?"

"Yes, walk. Now watch me, and then we'll do the walk together."

Sarah smiled to herself because Sifu was walking like a duck.

He said, "The first thing is to learn to tuck. This is very important because it helps your back and your inner organs, it takes the pressure away from your knees, and it helps your balance. When you become older, you'll be glad you learned to tuck." Then he told her how to relax the body into a tuck, letting the thigh take the pressure, not the knees. He began to slowly move his feet forward.

Then it was Sarah's turn. She found walking like a duck wasn't as easy as it looked.

Sifu said, "Keep walking and tuck. If you tuck, you are in constant line with the energy flow from the ground, but if you bob up and down, you break that connection."

Sarah walked backward and forward in the back of the room and tried not to bob. That was the beginning of her new way of thinking and moving her body.

When Sarah was going home with her mother, all Sarah could talk about was how interesting the lineage was and what she had learned that day. And did her mother know how hard it was to walk like a duck?

Each day, when anything went wrong at school, which it usually did, she would think of *Tai Chi*. At least there, her walks were improving. She was able to 'duck walk,' and maybe today was the day she would learn a new step. But of course that was up to Sifu. Sarah thought it was funny when she was corrected at school, it bothered her, but when Sifu corrected her, it was always done with the understanding that she would be able to do it correctly later on in another lesson.

When they had oral tests in school, Sarah was able to pass, but when anything was written down, she failed. She was good in sports, and everyone wanted her to be on their team. Those were good days, and Sarah loved to be able to help her team win. Now she had a secret, she was learning how to do something no one else in the whole school was doing. One of her goals was to be in the end-of-the-year talent contest and show everyone she could learn something, and do it well. But that wasn't until June, eight months later. She hoped she would be able to learn *Short Form* by then, but at the rate she was going, she wasn't so sure.

Chapter 5

When Sarah arrived at the *Tai Chi* school, she would go to the dressing room and put on her T-shirt, long black sweat pants, and her *Tai Chi* shoes. Then, she would hang her school uniform up and put her shoes and book-bag in her cubbyhole.

She thought of what Sifu had told her about how *Tai Chi* shoe soles were made. The Chinese people took rags and mixed them with certain paints, and when the process was over, they used this mixture to make the soles of the *Tai Chi* shoes. These soles really helped your feet slide easily into the next step. As she walked down the hall towards the classroom, she thought how smart the Chinese people were to invent this type of shoe.

Of all the students at this school, Sarah liked Monica the best. Monica was always there to help Sarah and never made fun of her. In fact, no one ever said a mean thing about anyone, in or out of the *Tai Chi* school. Sarah enjoyed being in the beginner's class.

Sifu said, "Just keep practicing and you'll get it." Sarah kept working on the new walks, and when she did it right, she knew, because she felt balanced.

Her new friends were always giving positive help, and that helped Sarah relax more and not worry about being perfect the first time she tried a new movement. Sarah loved everything about the school. The beginning warm-ups for the whole class were called, *Chi Gung*. Other exercises that helped with practicing your Forms were, *Silk Cocoon and Carry Tiger to the Mountain*. Sarah thought the class looked like a slow moving wave when they did *Carry Tiger to the Mountain*. Then Sarah would go to the back of the room and work on her walks, while the rest of the class began to work on *Short Form*. It was hard for Sarah to not watch the other students, but she told herself, *Someday I'll be able to do that too.*

She would try to remember not to look down when she walked, but straight ahead. Imagining an invisible pole, which she would straddle, helped, too, in doing the walk correctly. Weeks went by, and slowly Sarah learned a few more walks. They were not as easy as they looked. She kept telling herself, *Tuck, relax, and bend your arms a bit.* And at her regular school, she found it easier to play volleyball, because she was able to practice her tuck. Much to her surprise, it really helped when she went to spike the ball.

The greatest day for Sarah was when Sifu said, "Do you think you are ready for *Short Form?*" Sarah was so excited she couldn't say a word, but nodded her head. Sifu said, "I think you are ready too. Before we start, I'm going to show you how the *Palm Stance* is done. Watch me first, and then we will all do it together." He stood in front of the class and slowly raised his arms, making them look like a big circle. He stopped when he reached his chest. Then Sifu said, "You're going to relax your shoulders while your arms form a circle, and, of course, your body is in the tuck position." The class did the exercise with him.

Sweet, thought Sarah, as they stood there with their arms out in front, just relaxing. Sarah realized that if she pulled her fingertips away from each other, she was able to feel energy.

Doing this almost made her miss what Sifu said next. "Slowly bring your arms down to your side."

The next step was the beginning of the *Short Form*. Sarah had practiced the walks and thought that would be first, but they weren't. Sifu showed the class the first move, and then everyone began with him the second time. Sarah's arms came up slowly in front of her, and then bending her elbows, she pulled her arms towards her chest very slowly; the next step was to push slowly downward.

"Now go practice this step one hundred times," said Sifu.

The girls stood in front of the wall mirror and slowly began to move their arms the way they had been shown. Sarah thought this was wonderful, almost like being in water. After she practiced the new move a few times, she went back to practicing her walks.

Chapter 6

The weeks passed slowly while Sarah was in school. Georgia was always asking Mrs. Dominick, "Could I call out spelling words or questions for the test for Sarah?" Georgia's group always sat together at recess and lunch. They whispered, then giggled about someone in their class that had not done well that day. Sarah was always on the top of their list.

Sarah would try not to get upset. Then she would remember how far she had come in the *Short Form,* and that made her feel better.

Thanksgiving came and everyone was talking about where he or she would be going, or what he or she would be doing for the holiday. When the bell rang at three o'clock, everyone left the school building, yelling, "I'll see you next week," while running to their school buses and waiting cars. Sarah walked to her bus, climbed aboard, and sat in the front seat with a big smile on her face. There would be more time for *Tai Chi* during this short vacation, and she couldn't wait.

Thanksgiving vacation wasn't totally a happy time, however. Sarah just couldn't get this one new part of *Short Form.* She hadn't gone very far in the *Form* and hit a block she just couldn't pass. The more she practiced, the worse it got. She went over to the bench by the wall and watched everyone practicing.

Sifu asked, "What's wrong?"

Sarah said, "I'm just not getting this. Just like in school, I'm just not good enough."

Sifu said, "Remember what I told you when you began?"

Sarah nodded her head.

"Well," Sifu said, "you must want to learn *Tai Chi* and work very hard before you will be able to do it. Keep in mind that you will never finish learning *Tai Chi*; there is always something new, but on a different level. You go home after class and think about it. When you come back, we'll talk, Ok?"

Sarah said, "I'll try." She then began to practice again.

Sifu smiled to himself as he walked away thinking, *She just might make it.*

Chapter 7

Vacation ended sooner than Sarah wanted it to, and now she was back in school facing a written spelling test. She had studied over vacation with her mother and knew how to spell all the words. The problem was writing them down. Right after recess, the teacher said, "Everyone take out a sheet of paper for the spelling test." Mrs. Dominick began saying the words, first just the word, then the word in a sentence, and lastly just the word again.

Sarah spelled each word to herself and then wrote the word down on the paper. When the test was over, the students exchanged papers with the person next to them. Mrs. Dominick called out each word and someone in the class would spell the word correctly. When this was over, the checkers wrote the number of errors on the top of the paper, and then passed it to the front of the row, where a student would collect them and give them to Mrs. Dominick. Class droned on and finally it was three o'clock. Class was dismissed.

Sarah got up, collected her books and lunch box, and started towards the door. Mrs. Dominick said, "Sarah, I need to speak with you. Would you wait a few moments?"

Sarah turned, and Georgia was right in front of her smiling, saying, "Bet you failed your test again." Sarah just walked past her and went to the teacher's desk.

Mrs. Dominick said, "I know you have to catch your bus, but I want to have a conference with you and your mother. Here is a note asking your mother to come in on Friday morning before school." Sarah took the note and left the room, holding back tears. Now her mother would have to come in and it would make her late for work. *It's my fault,* thought Sarah. Nothing seemed to go right at school or at *Tai Chi.* It seemed like the harder she worked in both places, the worse she got. She had tried so hard and just couldn't seem to do well in school.

That day was a, *Mrs. Rogers day.* Mrs. Rogers was really nice and worked with Sarah on her spelling words. She told Sarah how to break words apart and that sometimes they made smaller words. She thought this might help Sarah do better on her next test. Mrs. Rogers asked, "Sarah, is there something wrong?"

Sarah said, "Yes, my teacher wants to see my mother and me on Friday. You know I try hard and get all of my homework done, but I just can't seem to write down the words correctly. Even my reading is not very good," complained Sarah.

Mrs. Rogers said, "Well, now that we know your problem, we'll just have to work on it."

Sarah's mother picked her up and they went home. That night after dinner, Sarah gave her mom the note from school. She said, "Mom, I am so sorry about you having to come to school and making you late for work."

Her mother said, "Don't worry, I'll ask if it would be alright if I come in a little late for work."

Friday morning came all too soon for Sarah. They met with Mrs. Dominick in her classroom. She showed Sarah's mom the grades and said, "If Sarah keeps going down this road, she will not pass school this year." She suggested that Mrs. Clarke hire a tutor for Sarah. Mrs. Dominic knew a wonderful retired teacher named Mrs. Rogers, who may be able to help.

Mrs. Clarke said, "Mrs. Rogers already takes care of Sarah after school three days a week. I'll talk with her tonight." Mrs. Clarke thanked Mrs. Dominick, then said good-bye to Sarah as she left the classroom.

Mrs. Dominick said, "Sarah, don't forget you have a spelling test today, and that you should study before school starts."

After school, Sarah went to *Tai Chi.* She felt better today about school, since she had made a C- on her spelling test. *Sweet!* She had used Mrs. Rogers' idea about taking some of the spelling words apart, and it worked.

Now she would work on improving her *Tai Chi* moves. She and Sifu had talked, and she told him that she would work hard to improve her attitude, because she was starting to feel the energy in her body. It wasn't much, but when she felt it, it was wonderful. The bad part was when she felt it, she got excited and lost her place during the moves.

Sifu said, "You will feel more energy as time goes on, but that will be sometime in the future. You must work on continuing to move even after you feel the energy. When you stop, you lose it, and it will take a few more moves until your energy returns to your body. Practice, practice. It all comes with practice."

Sarah thought, *Everything comes with practice,* and she sure was getting practice in everything she did.

Chapter 8

Sarah's spelling and reading were improving. Mrs. Rogers had given her some tests and found out she was *Dyslexic*. She had a problem with reading, math, and spelling. She wasn't dumb; she just had a learning problem. Now that she knew what was wrong, she would work with Mrs. Rogers on this problem. She knew she would never be an A-student, but she would work towards that goal anyway.

The next day Sarah went to *Tai Chi* class and asked to speak with Sifu alone. She began to speak, "Sifu, I have a learning problem and Mrs. Rogers is helping me." She also told him that it would not interfere with *Tai Chi* because there was no writing in *Tai Chi*, just movements. Now that that problem was cleared up, she would be able to concentrate better and not feel like half of her life was a failure.

Sifu answered, "We all have problems. When you're here, think of *Tai Chi* and let it become part of your life."

Sarah improved in school with the help of Mrs. Rogers. Sarah would take her spelling and math test with Mrs. Rogers, and then Mrs. Rogers would send the answers to Mrs. Dominick. That way, no one knew Sarah was taking her tests orally.

Georgia asked, "Mrs. Dominick, how come Sarah doesn't need help at recess anymore?"

Mrs. Dominick said, "Sarah is improving on her own without any help. Thank you for your concern." Mrs. Dominic then walked toward a group of students playing volleyball.

Sarah had some hard times in *Tai Chi* class and became frustrated about not getting certain moves like *Cloud Hands*. She just couldn't get the sliding of the feet and the hand movement; she always ended up with her hand too high, or putting her toe out instead of her heel first. The more she tried the worse it seemed to get. She would become frustrated with practicing the move again and again.

Sarah could hear Sifu's voice saying, "*Each time it is wrong, do it a hundred more times. You need to laugh at yourself, relax, take a break from that move, and begin the form again. That way you'll improve on the first part of* **The Form** *and feel the energy flow through your body.*"

Those were the days that Sarah wanted to quit. Then she would think about the flow of energy that she would sometimes feel, and she would begin to practice again. In her head, she would hear Sifu saying, "*Follow your hand movement in the direction you will be going, then look to where you will be moving. It all flows; one movement flows into the next.*" Sarah worked with the class up to the part she had not been taught, and then she would go to the back of the class and practice.

Sifu would come back to where she was practicing and say, "Tuck, Sarah, tuck!"

Sarah just couldn't get the knack of tucking. She knew she was bobbing and losing the energy, and this really upset her. But she knew she would get it; it was just a matter of time. Sarah thought, *One hundred times are a lot of times, but if that is what it takes, I'll do it!*

Chapter 9

In the next few months some new students joined the beginner's class, but only one stayed to continue working. Sarah remembered that Sifu had told her some people think it is easy to do, and when they find out it's hard work, they quit. It was hard, but she loved it. She knew that if you want something, you must work hard to achieve it. And boy, was she working hard! It seemed like when she learned something new, she would go home to practice it and she wouldn't get it right. So she would begin *The Form* again. Once in a while she did remember. The next time in class, she would ask Sifu to show her again, knowing he would say, *"Practice is the answer. Do it a hundred more times."*

Sarah loved the different names of the movements; there was *Snake Creeps Down, White Crane,* and *Cloud Hands*. She thought *Snake Creeps Down* was hard because your feet moved first, then your hands moved, then your feet moved, and finally your belly button had to be facing the direction that your left hand was pointing. Topping this off was the release of power that your left hand pushes out. Boy, was that one hard to learn, and of course, still needed practice.

Sifu said, "Watch me as I do *Snake Creeps Down*." He talked about what he was doing with his hands and feet. "You move your feet and arm because you are deflecting an attack with the left arm, then your left arm comes up and strikes your opponent. You must always be ready to deflect a blow. If you are not tucked and ready, you will end up being hurt." Then he told the class to do this three times. He walked around and made small corrections with each student. Sarah liked the way Sifu corrected her. He would only give you two corrections, even though you knew you had a lot more wrong with your form. He said that since students are not able to correct everything immediately, he'd just work on a few things at a time.

Sarah would watch Sifu as they all did *Short Form,* and each time, she saw something new that she should have learned. She asked Sifu, "Did I just miss it or was I not practicing it correctly?"

Sifu said, "No, you will always see and learn more in the *Short Form,* but keep practicing. Remember to practice, practice, and you will continually learn more about *Tai Chi.*"

Chapter 10

Christmas vacation was only two days away, and all the students in Mrs. Dominick's class were going on a field trip to the museum in the next city. Hal was the bus driver, and Sarah said hello as she made her way to one of the seats. Georgia and her friends got on and sat in the back. Sarah was glad they did. That way she wouldn't have to listen to them talk about people.

The forty-five minute trip went by quickly, with everyone talking and singing Christmas carols. When the bus stopped, Mrs. Dominick said, "Now I would like everyone to have a partner, and you will stay with that person for the entire visit in the museum."

Sarah was sitting next to Rita and asked, "Will you be my partner?" Rita was a very quiet girl and nodded her head. Rita and Sarah stood outside the bus in line waiting for everyone. Finally, Georgia and her friends climbed off and walked to the front of the line, right behind Mrs. Dominick.

As they entered the museum, Sarah turned to Rita and said, "Look at the ceiling, it's painted to look like the night sky." Some of the students looked up too, and before long the whole class had stopped to look.

Mrs. Dominick said, "Class, you have to move over to the side of the entrance, because you are blocking the way for other visitors." Mrs. Dominick then introduced John to the class and said he would be their guide. The rest of the morning was spent seeing wonderful exhibits from all over the world.

When lunchtime came, they went outside and sat on large benches to eat their lunch. Everyone was talking about all the wonderful things they had seen and taken notes on. Sarah had her notebook open and was trying to write a note on the last exhibit she had seen, when a shadow crossed over her page. She stopped and looked up in time to see Georgia reading what she had written.

Georgia giggled and said, "How can you make sense out of what you have just written, when you can't even spell half of the words?" Sarah closed her book and put it down beside her lunch box and did not say a word.

Georgia and her friends sat on the benches behind Sarah and Rita, eating their lunch. When Sarah picked up her lunch box, she didn't notice that her notebook had slipped backward. As she and Rita began to eat their lunches, they heard the girls' giggles turn into laughter and mimic the spelling of certain words.

Sarah turned and realized Georgia was reading her notebook. She put her sandwich down and walked over to their table and said, "May I please have my notebook?"

Georgia said, "What notebook?"

Sarah reached for the book, and as she did, a fist came towards her. Without thinking, Sarah deflected the punch and heard a scream. One of Georgia's friends had tried to punch Sarah in the arm, but Sarah's reflex was too quick. Sarah had knocked Jenny on the ground before either girl knew what had happened.

Georgia yelled, "Mrs. Dominic, Sarah knocked Jenny down!"

When Mrs. Dominick arrived, Sarah was helping Jenny up off the ground.

Georgia said, "For no reason at all, Sarah came over to our table and tried to grab one of our brownies, and Jenny tried to stop her. That is when Sarah hit Jenny so hard it knocked her back over the bench."

Mrs. Dominick asked both girls to come with her. Georgia tried to come too, but was told to stay where she was.

Mrs. Dominick said, "Now girls, we will not be able to clear this up here, so both of you will sit in the front seat of the bus on the way home." Mrs. Dominick turned towards the class and said, "Everyone should have finished lunch by now. Clean up the area where you were sitting, then line up with your partner to get back on the bus."

Sarah and Jenny returned to where they had sat and helped clean up. As everyone got on the bus, they were all talking about the fight, not the museum! Hal wondered what happened and who was in the fight. When he found out it was Sarah, he was surprised. He knew she would not start a fight. There was something wrong with this whole situation.

The ride home was a quiet one, and before the students got off the bus, Mrs. Dominick said, "Class, you have been very good, of course, with one exception. Now class, go back into school and to the classroom, quietly." Mrs. Dominick then turned to Sarah and Jenny and said, "Both of you will come to the Principal's office with me."

Mrs. Dominick told the girls to sit in the outer office, while she went to talk to the Principal, Mr. Price. After a few moments, Mrs. Dominick opened the office door and told the girls to go in. Then she went back to her classroom.

Both girls sat in chairs in front of Mr. Price's desk, with their hands folded in their laps. Mr. Price asked, "Jenny, what happened?"

Jenny said, "Sarah came over to my table and tried to grab my things. You can ask the other girls at my table."

Mr. Price then asked Sarah, "Now you tell me what happened." As Sarah told her side of the story, Jenny kept trying to interrupt, saying that Sarah's story wasn't true.

Mr. Price listened, then said, "You both go sit in the chairs outside of my office." Mr. Price left his office and went to Mrs. Dominick's room. Mrs. Dominick came to the door of her room and stepped outside into the hallway. They spoke for a few moments.

It was almost time for the bell to ring, and the students had all of their lunch boxes sitting on their desks. Georgia was telling everyone how Sarah was so stupid and now she even hit someone.

Doug, one of the boys, stood up in class and told everyone to stop talking about what happened. "It's not anyone's business." Turning to Georgia, he said, "Especially you."

Georgia sat down and pouted, mumbling under her breath, "We'll see who gets in trouble."

When Mrs. Dominick returned to the room, she said, "Suzie and Rita take Sarah's and Jenny's lunchboxes and jackets to the office and come right back to the room, because the bell is going to ring."

Chapter 11

Sarah and Jenny's mothers came to school and went into Mr. Price's office. Both girls waited with their heads down, not looking at each other. When their mothers came out of the office, Mr. Price was behind them, and no one was smiling.

Sarah's mother came to her and said, "Let's go home and talk." Sarah sat in the front seat of the car and stared quietly out the window.

When they were inside the house, Sarah told her mother what had happened and that she was sorry. Her mother said, "Both you and Jenny are not to go back to school tomorrow. That means both of you will miss the Christmas party and saying good-bye to your friends. You will be able to go back when school re-opens on January 2nd."

Sarah said, "Where will I go tomorrow?"

Her mother said, "I'll call Mrs. Rogers and ask if she will be able to watch you for the day."

Sarah helped fix dinner. It was a quiet dinner, with only a few words spoken. After dinner, Sarah washed and dried the dishes, then went to her room. She couldn't understand how her reflexes were so fast. Gee, she hoped if someone reached in front of her, she wouldn't knock them down. She would have to talk to Sifu about this new problem.

During the Christmas holidays, Sarah continued her *Tai Chi* classes. Her first day back, she asked Sifu if she could ask him a question.

He said, "Would after class be alright?"

Sarah said, "That would be fine." After class, Sifu and Sarah sat on a bench in the classroom, and Sarah began to ask about her quick reflexes.

Sifu said, "Hold it. What happened to make you defend yourself?" Sarah told him the story about what happened on the field trip and its outcome.

Sifu nodded and then said, "You should not be afraid of your reactions. You felt in danger and your body told you to protect yourself. I know you wouldn't just knock someone down. You have become more aware of your surroundings. That is all part of *Tai Chi*, getting in touch with your inner self." Sarah understood, but not why someone would want to hit her, when they were in the wrong for taking her book.

Sifu said, "There are all types of people in this world. You must listen to your body's instincts. They will keep you on the right path."

The holidays flew by, and before Sarah knew it, it was time to go back to school. Sarah told her mother about the talk with Sifu.

Sarah's mother said, "I love you, Sarah. I also believe your account of what happened at the museum." Sarah's mom had come to her room and said, "Hold your head up tomorrow. Things will work out for you."

Sarah climbed on the bus the next morning, said hello to Hal, then went and sat down in a seat by the window. When she got off the bus, Hal said, "Have a nice day Sarah."

Sarah smiled and walked into the school building saying, "It's water over the dam and I will not hold a grudge. "

School went by quickly, and Sarah couldn't understand why. Then she realized, Georgia wasn't in school. She was home sick with the Chickenpox. So for the next two weeks, school was great and Sarah was passing her tests with C minuses. Her *Tai Chi* classes were hard, but also improving. Now she was learning *Four Corners,* and it was really hard. She had to move her hands and feet to north corner, then move back turning to the west corner on the other side of the room, south came next and last was east. She just couldn't get the part of which hand went where and ended up in the wrong place. Some of the other girls caught on and were doing well. It seemed the harder Sarah tried, the worse she got.

Sifu came over and told her to begin the *Short Form* again. "First stand and gather energy. Let your body fall into a tuck, and let the energy flow through. Then begin *The Form* again." Sarah stood there with her eyes closed and felt the energy slowly come up through the ground. It was only a little, but enough to let her forget everything but breathing. That is important. She remembered Sifu telling her, "Clear your mind, tuck, and concentrate on your breathing." She always had a hard time clearing her mind; everything that happened that day or was happening in the class was running through her mind.

Today she relaxed, tucked, thought of darkness, and then her breath in this darkness. She could feel the energy. It was a wonderful feeling! Opening her eyes, she slowly brought her hands down and began *The Form*. She moved slowly, feeling the energy being pulled up from the ground. In her *Form,* she felt like she was in water pushing and pulling, a feeling she had never felt before. When she came to the *Four Corners,* she had some problems, but made it through.

Sifu came over and smiled. "Now practice it a hundred times and remember to tuck."

Chapter 12

Georgia came back to school, but the classroom had changed while she was gone. The students didn't listen to Georgia as much, now telling her to be quiet when she started to talk about another student. Her group of friends had gotten smaller too. Jenny was the first one to leave her group. In fact, she had gone to the Principal and told him it was all her fault at the museum, not Sarah's. What surprised Sarah even more was when Jenny came over to her on the playground and said, "Sarah, I am sorry for trying to punch you at the picnic."

Sarah realized that the school year was coming to an end in two months. She wondered if she would be ready for the talent show. In *Tai Chi* class, she worked very hard, and like everyone who takes any type of martial arts, practiced at home as well. Sarah was almost finished with *Short Form*; now there were only two more sections to learn. She knew she would have to continue to work on it even when she finished the *Form*. Now she understood Sifu's words: "You will always learn something new each time you practice; you must continue to practice, whether it's on your breathing, hands, legs, or having your body in the correct position."

The big end-of-year tests were coming up too. The outcome of these tests determined whether students passed or failed the school year. Sarah was getting nervous about the tests, and she talked to Mrs. Rogers about her feelings. Mrs. Rogers said, "Maybe something can be done about them. I will check into it."

Sarah continued to practice her *Tai Chi* and homework each day. She now knew she was not dumb, and hoped she would pass the test so she would be able to go to sixth grade next year.

Georgia hadn't talked to Sarah very much, but this day she came over and asked, "Are you going to be in the talent show?"

Sarah said, "I'm not sure."

Georgia said, "Don't waste your time on entering, because I've won the last few years and I'll win this time too." Then, as she walked away, she said over her shoulder, "I'm just warning you, give up the idea, because you'll lose."

Time flew by and Sarah finished *Short Form*. But she still practiced it each day, both at *Tai Chi* School and at home. She asked Sifu, "Will you watch me and tell me where I need to improve?"

Sifu smiled and said, "Any part?"

Sarah nodded her head, and asked Sifu if she was ready to show people the *Short Form* in a contest?

Sifu asked, "Do you think you are ready?"

Sarah said, "Yes!"

"Good. Then I'll help you. But remember: This is only the beginning. Practice this *Form* daily, even when you move on to the next *Form.*"

One week before the show, the talent applications were handed out to any student who wanted to enter the contest. Sarah took one of the sheets and began to fill it out. Georgia came over to her desk, put her hands on her hips, and said, "I told you it was a waste of your time, but if you want to look stupid, that's your problem." Sarah looked up at Georgia and just smiled, then finished filling out the sheet. Georgia walked away in a huff.

The night before the show, Sarah's mom gave her a package after dinner. Sarah asked, "What is this?"

Her mother winked at her. Sarah tore open the package and held a brand new *Tai Chi* uniform close to her chest, and then hugged her mom. "Thank you, Mom! How did you know what I wanted?"

Her mom just laughed.

Chapter 13

The next morning, Sarah took her book bag to school, even though there were no books inside. What was inside was her *Tai Chi* outfit and shoes. Her mother had braided Sarah's blond hair, so it hung down her back and would be out of the way when she preformed *Tai Chi*.

In school, Mrs. Dominick called the class to order, and then said, "Test results are in and I am very proud of everyone." Sarah sat there with her fingers crossed; right now passing to the sixth grade was the most important thing in her life.

Mrs. Dominick said, "You will receive your report cards at the end of the day." Sarah didn't think she could stand not knowing about the outcome for the entire school day. But she would have to wait.

She tried to put the test score in the back of her mind; there was nothing she could do anyway. There was a classroom party and everyone signed each other's autograph books. Spirits were high, and the students were enjoying themselves when the announcement came over the intercom, "All participants in the talent contest please come to the auditorium." The room went quiet as both Georgia and Sarah rose to go to the auditorium. The students called out good luck to the girls.

Neither girl said anything all the way down the hall until they entered the auditorium. Then Sarah said, "Good luck Georgia," before she turned towards the girls' room to change into her outfit.

Mr. Fisher told the contestants to go backstage and sit in the seats provided. Mrs. Murphy was holding a large basket, telling the students that the basket was filled with numbers. "The number you choose is the order in which you will perform." There were fifteen students, and Sarah drew number twelve.

Mr. Price came backstage and said, "Everyone, I am proud of each student and wish you all good luck. Remember after your performance, you are to go to the other side of the back stage. Stay there until all the students have preformed. The winners will be called out on stage to get their ribbons."

The auditorium began to fill with students, teachers, and parents, as those backstage sat thinking about their routines. The numbers were called slowly, and finally it was Georgia's turn. She had on a beautiful dress and looked like a little doll. Her talent was singing, and she sang a new pop tune. Everyone clapped and whistled as she bowed and walked to the other side of the stage.

Then it was Sarah's turn; she had been sitting in her seat practicing her breathing. Sarah's music started, and everyone became very quiet as she walked out on stage. Sarah did her stance with her arms out, collecting energy. She felt it slowly coming up through the stage floor, and then she lowered her arms and began *Short Form*. She was in a world of her own, with *Chi* she had never felt before. This wonderful feeling ran throughout her body, almost like she was in water, pushing and pulling and feeling the energy. When she came to the end, she slowly let her arm come down and she shook out the last bit of *Chi*, then bowed and left the stage. The auditorium was totally quiet. Then it erupted into applause and cheers. Sarah sat down and put her head in her hands. She had never felt the *Chi* like she had just experienced, and hoped she would be able to feel it again. It was just too wonderful to let go!

The winning students were called, starting with fifth place. Sarah didn't care if she won or not. Nothing could make her any happier than what she had just experienced. Sarah heard Georgia's name being called and thought she had won first place, but it was second place. Then Mr. Price came backstage, took Sarah's hand and brought her out on stage. He announced, "Sarah Clark has won first place!" Everyone cheered, and as Sarah looked out into the audience, she saw her mother. Beside her were Mrs. Rogers and Sifu Jon. Sarah could only smile.

On the way back to the classroom, Sarah noticed Georgia had fallen back from the class and had her head down. Sarah slowed down until Georgia was beside her. Sarah said quietly "I think your voice is really beautiful."

Back in the classroom everyone congratulated Sarah and wanted to know all about *Tai Chi*. Sarah said, "You will have to go to the *Tai Chi* School, Sifu can explain it a lot better than I can."

Mrs. Dominick said, "I have enjoyed teaching you this year and hope you all have a happy summer. As each child left the room, she handed them "The Envelope" and then said good-bye. When she handed Sarah her envelope, she winked and said, "Have a wonderful summer, *sixth grader.*"

Chapter 14

"You want me to do what!" exclaimed Judy.

Sarah was laughing so hard at the expression on Judy's face that it took her a moment to answer the question. "Yes, we all go into the ocean on New Year's Day. It's really fun. First, Sifu and some of the older members make this big wood fire on the beach. We all stand around it, dressed in our bathing suits and tennis or beach shoes. Sifu tells us to hold hands and think of last year, things that we wanted to do but didn't, or anything else that bothered us. With our heads down, holding hands, we think about this," Sarah said.

Sifu says, "Wipe these thoughts away from your minds." We turn towards the ocean, making a long line, and run into the waves. You must go completely under the water and run out again towards the bonfire. Afterwards, we go home and take a shower, dress in warm clothes, and then take a potluck dish back to the Club Center, where everyone sits around and talks about the day.

Judy was still not convinced about going into the ocean. "Sarah, the ocean is forty-two degrees and to me, that is freezing. I'll be an ice-cube and won't be able to get out of the water."

Sarah said, "Everyone holds hands and helps anyone that needs help out of the ocean. You really don't feel the cold water because you run in and quickly drop down and get your head wet, and then run out. The cold part is the wind, if it is blowing. Besides, my mom will be there holding big beach towels to wrap around us."

Judy thought a moment and then laughed, "Well if you can do it, so can I. Besides, there are a few things that I didn't get done this year and I want to make a fresh start next year. You're on!"

Chapter 15

The next day, Sarah told Sifu that Judy would be joining them on the New Year's Day Plunge. Sifu laughed and turned towards Judy and nodded.

Judy had joined the Club Center in August where she had met Sarah and they become friends. Sarah watched Judy practice her walks and would remember the hard time she had learning them. She and Judy would laugh about the walks and practice them together when they were at Mrs. Rogers' home. Mrs. Rogers made sure the girls had their homework done before they were able to practice.

Christmas came and went before anyone realized the plunge was scheduled for the following day. Judy spent the night at Sarah's home, so they would be sure to be at the beach on time. Sifu had posted the time and place for everyone to meet on January 1st. Sarah's mom knew just where and when to take the girls that day.

The girls woke up and got dressed in their bathing suits and sweat suits. They sat around the breakfast table, eating and talking about the events of the day.

Sarah said, "What are you cooking for the potluck, Mom?"

"Chili."

Twelve o'clock was the magic hour and the girls wanted to be there early, so they arrived at eleven. Sarah put her camera, their towels, and beach shoes into the car. They felt the warm sun and chilly breeze as they climbed out of the car.

"I can't believe I am doing this," Judy kept saying as they walked down to the beach.

Sifu and some of the older members had placed the bonfire high up on the beach, so the incoming tide would not reach the fire. Some club members were sitting on the large pieces of driftwood nearby talking about the plunge. Sarah and Judy saw Lynne and Joanna and went over to talk to them.

The time came and everyone joined hands around the fire with their heads bowed. This was the time for reflection. Sifu said, "Everyone hold hands and when I say ok, we'll run towards the water together." Then he called out, "OK."

Everyone began to run towards the water, laughing. Sarah and Judy held hands and began to run with the group. Judy's first steps into the icy water made her want to turn around and run back out. She called to Sarah, "I can't do it."

"It will be over before you know it," Sarah said, as they continued to run into the water laughing about how far it was to the deep water. Then out of nowhere, a big wave hit both girls, knocking them down. Sarah jumped up, grabbed Judy, and they both ran shivering back up the beach to the fire.

Sarah called to her mother, "Where are the towels?"

Her mom answered, "Right here on my arms. You both are so cold you can't stop shivering long enough to see them."

The girls ran to the bonfire and stood next to Lynne and Joanna as they were all trying to get warm. Sarah pointed to some of the people around the fire and said, "See, we all look as though we are steaming." Everyone laughed and nodded.

Sifu said, "Everyone go home and take a hot bath, then meet back at the Club Center."

The tables at the club were brimming over with food. Jaime and Tristram were sitting in the corner talking about being first in the ocean, while Jeff argued he was first. Sarah, Judy, Lynne, and Joanna were saying they didn't realize how cold the plunge was, and the funny things that had happened at the beach. One of the boys had lost his trunks when he dove into a wave.

After the party, Sarah's mom took Judy home. Sarah called out of the window, "See you in school tomorrow."

Chapter 16

Sarah had to present a project for the science fair that morning, so her mother had driven her to school. She walked down the hall holding the large display tightly in front of her, when a door suddenly swung open, hitting her, and knocking the assignment onto the floor. Sarah stood looking at all the pieces of her display, some were broken while others were torn.

When she looked up, her eyes met Georgia's. "Oh, I didn't know anyone was outside the door," Georgia said.

Sarah held her temper and said, "Accidents happen." Georgia walked on down the hall humming a tune.

"What happened Sarah?" asked her science teacher.

"There was an accident in the hallway. Hopefully I'll be able to put it back together before the science fair." Then Sarah laughed, "At least the written report wasn't damaged."

Class started and Sarah was the first to present her assignment to the class. There were giggles as she brought her display to the front table. One of the students asked, "What happened to it?"

"I dropped it." Sarah had put her exhibit back together, but it still looked like a tornado had hit it. Sarah had memorized her report, and as she spoke, she would point to the different parts of the project. At first, there were giggles when she would point to a broken part, but soon there were no giggles, only interest in what she was saying.

Sarah's report was about the importance of eating food from organic farms. All of the science projects were to be placed on tables in the gym where they would be judged. Each child had to stand by theirs and answer any questions that the judges might ask.

Judy noticed how nervous Sarah was so she told Sarah, "Don't worry about anything. Your report was really good." Then she asked, "What happened to your project?" Sarah told her the story. But before Judy could ask anything else, one of the judges began to ask questions about Sarah's project.

"I see yours is on organic farming, do you eat organic food?"

"Yes sir, we always try to eat organic foods when we can." Mr. Holtz asked a few more questions and then moved on to the next student.

After school, Sarah's bus dropped her off at the *Tai Chi* building. She dressed, then went into the classroom and began some warm-ups before starting to practice her new moves. Sarah was working on her *Long Form* when her old problem of not tucking slid back into her *Form*. She thought about Sifu reminding her to find the core in her body. She continued to practice with a smile on her face and let her hips drop down with her knees bent just a bit. *There, I now am able to feel balance.*

As Sifu walked into classroom, everyone stopped what they were doing and said, "Good afternoon Sifu." He nodded and went to the front of the room and began the *Chi Gong* warm ups. These are exercises to warm up each part of your body from head to toe before you begin the different *Forms*. The class then began *Short Form* slowly. The slower you do this *Form* the harder it is.

After Short Form, Sifu talked about three corrections that should be practiced. "Remember: Do not break your wrist. Keep it so there is flow in your movements, look towards the directions you will be moving just before you make those moves, and breathe." He showed how to improve each problem, and then everyone did these corrections three times on their own.

Sarah kept telling herself to tuck and not to bob up and down when she was doing the form. She must remember to keep at one height throughout the from, When Sarah's part of the from was completed, Sifu once again made corrections, specifically for her.

Sifu asked, "Sarah, did you *feel* your body in the tuck position?"

Sarah answered, "No, I tried to keep telling myself to, but I'm still having trouble."

Sifu said, "Remember, if you make a mistake, continue on. Do not break the flow of energy. Now practice that one hundred times."

Sarah went to the back of the room and began to practice her walks, since that's where one begins with finding the center of their body. If she couldn't do the walks without this, she would need even more practice. She thought, *Today was not a good day for me. First my project was wrecked, and now I'm having trouble with this. I thought I had it, but when I have problems at school, it just seems to come back.*

Chapter 17

The next week was a nightmare for Sarah. It seemed like everything she did, turned out wrong. She told herself, *I must concentrate more on what I'm doing.* It seemed the harder she worked, the worse it got. Then, out of the blue, when she was in *Tai Chi* class on Friday, it hit her. *Breathe! Stand and relax, gather energy, and breathe. How could I have forgotten the most important part of Tai Chi?*

Monday was report card day, and Sarah wasn't too sure what her grades were going to be. She had an idea they would all be Cs, but her science grade was what she was worried about. Her homeroom teacher handed out the report cards at the end of the day, and she held her breath when she received hers. She didn't open it, just put it in her book bag, and when the bell rang she walked out of school to her bus. She wasn't going to open it until she was alone. By the time it was her stop, she had decided to look when she got to *Tai Chi* school.

Sarah walked into the dressing room, then sat on the bench and opened her book bag. There it was the white folded report card. She pulled it out and looked, all C's. She started to close the card; when she saw her science grade, it was a B! She couldn't believe it. The teacher had written a note telling her that her science project was very good, and had brought her grade up to a B.

Sarah dressed for class and went into the classroom. She stood in front of the mirrored wall and practiced the part of *Long Form* that she had learned so far. When it was time to begin class, Sarah told herself, breathe, relax, and tuck. She felt energy in her body and was so excited about it that she lost her place. But she remembered what Sifu had told her, "Continue with the *Form*, do not lose the energy."

The class began *Long Form*, and when Sarah got to the part that she hadn't been taught, she moved to the back of the room and began to practice the *Forms* again. She would choose one correction to concentrate on each time. This time it was making sure her feet slid to the next position by not picking up her foot. That way, she would not lose the energy. Sarah remembered, each time that you practice, you should choose one thing to work on. That way you will improve your form.

Sifu came to the back of the room where Sarah was practicing *Long Form* and asked, "Are you ready to learn the next move in *Long Form?*"

Sarah nodded.

The new move is called *Needle At Sea Bottom*. "Watch me, and then we'll do it together." As Sarah watched, she thought it was a sweet new move.

Sifu said, "Now practice it three times, then go back to the beginning of the *Form* and add your new move. Then practice the *Form* again three more times."

Chapter 18

Sarah found that her reflexes were becoming quicker. When she played volleyball, she was faster at spiking the ball. Yesterday, Campbell had slammed her books on the desk and one of them started to fall off the pile; Sarah had caught it before it hit the floor. At that moment, Sarah realized that her awareness of things around her was becoming a little more in tune.

But schoolwork was becoming harder due to the demands of being a sixth grader. Spelling and math homework was taking longer to learn. In science class that day, Sarah's worst nightmare happened. Mr. Johnson had put cards with numbers printed on them in a bowl, then handed every other student a card with a number. The students without a card were to go up and draw a card, and find the student with the matching number. Almost everyone was happy with their new lab partner. Sarah's partner was Georgia. They just looked at one another, not believing what just happened.

Georgia said, "Mr. Johnson, I want another partner."

Mr. Johnson said, "I'm sorry, it wouldn't be fair to the other students if I let you do that."

Georgia sat down with a huff next to Sarah.

Mr. Johnson told everyone to take out their notebooks to begin to take notes. Mrs. Rogers had explained to Mr. Johnson about Sarah's learning problem, so when Sarah put the small tape recorder on the table, he just nodded.

Georgia called out, "Sarah is cheating. She has tape recorder and that isn't fair. Sarah isn't taking notes; she's using a tape recorder instead."

Mr. Johnson said that it was all right to take notes that way. But the notes had better be in her notebook when he checked them on Thursday. He told the class they were allowed to use a tape recorder, but they would be responsible for putting the information in their own notebook.

After school, Sarah headed towards her bus when Tristram asked if he would be able to borrow her tapes. Sarah said, "Yes, but it will have to be tomorrow morning, because I have to write the notes in my notebook first."

Chapter 19

The students became used to Sarah's tape recorder and would often ask her if they could listen to it after they had been absent from class. Sara told Mr. Johnson about this. Mr. Johnson asked the principal about having tapes on file in the library for students to use when they were absent from school. The idea was put into motion and the students thought it was great to have the class notes they missed on file for their use.

Georgia was, at least, talking to Sarah in science class now. Mr. Johnson said, "The duties of the lab equipment are to be shared. If one student takes out the equipment their partner puts it away, both shares the clean up of the table."

Georgia was good with the drawing, but didn't want to dissect anything or touch anything dead. Sarah said, "I can do that, if you'll help me draw the pictures."

Sarah was enjoying school more and her *Tai Chi* class was the highlight of her day. To her surprise, she realized that there was more to each move in both *Short* and *Long Form.* She now realized the slightest move of her hips, helped lead the body into the next position of the form. The eyes followed the movements, but just before you finished that move, your eyes were already looking in the direction of your next move. The classes helped her slow down with her schoolwork. She used to be in such a hurry to complete things, now she would check her work to make sure that it was neat and correct.

Judy and Sarah always met at lunchtime and talked about what had happened in their different classes. On test days, they would help each other to review their notes. Judy was now learning more moves in *Short Form* and, of course that was the topic of their conversation on the way to Club Center.

One day, Sarah and Judy entered Club Center and saw a group of girls and boys sitting on the benches outside Sifu's office. When the girls entered their class, the new girls were standing in the back of the room. Sarah and Judy bowed, then entered the practice room, said, "Hello" to the new girls, and then went to another area to practice.

Sifu had always said that, "When you enter the training room, do not stand around, but practice what you need to work on."

When Sifu entered the room, everyone, said, "Good afternoon, Sifu."

He nodded, and said, "We have three new members." Kierland, Caitlyn, and Campbell were introduced to the class, then warm up exercises began. Sifu reminded the class, "Hold your arms out with your elbow lower than hands, your body relaxed into a tuck. Remember, a string is pulling your head up and your back is straight, so the flow of energy moves up through your body."

Sarah loved this part of the warm-up because she was able to really feel the energy circling around her outstretched arms, while the fingers of each hand pulled away, then back towards each other making the pull of energy tug at her fingertips. Sometimes she was so intent during this exercise that she wouldn't hear Sifu's command to slowly take the hands down.

Class ended with *Ba Qua* (Everyone is in a circle and a tree or an object is placed in the center. The class moves in one direction doing the first palm and then go the other way doing the same thing.) Afterwards everyone bows, and then the oldest student goes up and shakes hands with Sifu and says, "Thank you."

This day, Sifu said, "I want your attention." The club had been asked to perform *The Lion Dance* for the opening of a Chinese restaurant. The older boys were going to have the honor of dancing with the lion costumes, but he needed some students to beat the drum, hit the cymbals, and ring the bells. "After class, I will have a sign up sheet for those who want to participate in the event."

Sarah and Judy were just about to leave the room when the three new girls walked over to them and introduced themselves. They began to ask questions about the practice room. What was the big seal on the wall, what were those bags hanging down in the room, why were there long sticks in holders, and why were there swords on the wall?

Sarah said, "Wait, let me go around the room slowly and explain what some of the things are used for. Let's start at the door. When you enter the practice room you bow like this." Sarah and Judy showed them the bow. Campbell asked, "Why?"

"To show respect to the practice area. Remember you are here to learn and respect others, not to hurt anyone." Sarah continued, "Next we have a silhouette of a person on the wall. The other class of Kung Fu uses that for practice. Sifu will explain about that, the hanging bags, long sticks, body pads and helmets. Also about the seal. I can tell you about the Lions that are mounted on the platforms on the wall. The black one is a *War Dragon* and the big yellow one is used for the *Lion Dance*. That was what Sifu was talking about when he said he needed students to volunteer to be the band for the *Lion Dance*."

The three girls looked up at the large yellow papier-mâché lion and Sarah told them it was a Mandarin Lion. "The large pink one is a girl dragon, and the colorful one with the horn in the middle of its head is a boy dragon. Two people are in each dragon, they move inside the covering of the dragon to make it look like the dragon is dancing."

Sarah and Judy said, "We have to leave and sign up for the performance." Sifu told the girls what instrument they would be playing. Judy would play the cymbals and Sarah the big drum. Sifu told them the times for practice and gave each student a permission slip to be signed by a parent by the next class meeting.

On the way home, Sarah told her mother about the demo and hoped she would be able to join the group.

Her mother said, "We will discuss it after dinner." Of course, dinner seemed to take forever. Finally, dinner was over and the table cleared. As Sarah entered the kitchen with the last of the dinner dishes, her mother said, "Maybe we can talk about the demo as we wash the dishes."

Sarah immediately began telling her mother about *The Lion Dance* and the band that would be playing as the lion danced. She said, "Judy and I could be part of the band, if you and Judy's mom agree."

"Only if your school work is completed. I'll talk with Sifu about my concerns."

Sarah asked, "When will you talk to him?"

Her mother said, "Don't worry about it, I'm sure that something can be worked out, but remember school comes first."

Sarah agreed and went to her room to work on her homework. Tomorrow she would have an English test and she needed to brush up on the parts of speech.

The next day at school, Sarah told Judy that she would have to wait until her mom talked to Sifu about the demo.

Judy said, "That it is what my mother said too."

The bell rang and both girls went to their classes. Judy called, "Good luck on your test."

Sarah waved and called back, "See you at lunch."

The test was hard, but Sarah thought she had passed. Mr. Roberts had a sweet way of giving his tests. He would hand out a blank sheet of paper, with his initials in the corner, to each student as they entered the room. Each student could write down anything they wanted to remember and then be able to use this sheet during the test. Sarah wrote down the parts of speech and a key word next to each part.

Mr. Roberts said, "It helps take the edge off being nervous." He would always collect both sheets as the student left the room. Sarah loved this idea and it really helped her. She wished other teachers would do this too.

After school, Sarah and Judy found out from Sifu that they were able to be in the band. Sifu said, "School always comes first. I know you won't disappoint your mothers or me."

Practice was at seven o'clock on Tuesdays and Thursdays. Mrs. Rogers was the one person that decided whether the girls would be able to go or not. Homework was checked and then she would drive the girls to practice. Mrs. Rogers really enjoyed watching the practice and the girls loved having her there. The three of them would joke about what happened at practice on the way back to her home.

Mrs. Rogers said, "I guess you'll need to practice the drum and cymbals just like your homework. Guess it won't be quiet around my house for a while." They all laughed.

Chapter 20

The day of the *Lion Dance,* the girls were dressed in their *Tai Chi* uniforms, with their long hair braided down their backs. Their mothers and Mrs. Rogers were seated in a good spot to take pictures of the dance and of the girls playing their instruments. Even though the girls had seen the practice, it was still wonderful to watch the performance. The lions were really funny, trying to get lettuce from the front of the overhang of the restaurant. They made a big mess, dropping lettuce all over the ground when they pretended to eat it. When the lions eat the lettuce, it brings good luck for the restaurant.

After the ceremony, Mr. Wong said, "Everyone is invited to come inside and eat lunch." All the performers were surprised and thanked Mr. and Mrs. Wong as they entered the restaurant.

Regular school was becoming interesting with all the class changes and different teachers. Sarah's math class was the hardest. She just couldn't understand the symbols and how they represented numbers.

Mr. Peterson said Sarah would need more practice and he would send some worksheets home with her. The practice helped, and she knew that she would have to memorize the rules.

In her other classes, she was receiving average grades but learning more than the tests showed. In science class, she and Georgia were becoming a team; each one helped the other complete the assignment and study for tests.

Georgia said, "Lets go over everything that I've written down." Sarah still had the tape recorder, but Georgia wanted to make sure Sarah would be able to understand the tapes better. When class was over, they both went their separate ways. Sarah didn't mind and just smiled to herself when Georgia ignored her in the hallways.

In *Tai Chi,* Sarah's new moves were, *Carry Tiger to Mountain* then into *Four Corners. Cloud Hands* followed this. Sarah had these moves before, but being in a new form, it felt different. She practiced these moves three times, and then began the whole *Form* again. All the *Forms* were done in sections and this helped her remember what move followed next.

Sarah liked the routine she followed each day, it really helped her keep organized. From *Tai Chi* she would go to Mrs. Rogers' and then do homework. Mrs. Rogers was helpful with ideas on studying. Sarah told her about Georgia and how she acted in class and in the hallways.

Mrs. Rogers smiled and said, "Georgia is trying to be kind, but just doesn't know how. You just keep doing what you have been, and Georgia may change towards you someday."

School was zooming by and Sarah once again heard about the talent contest. In science class, she asked, "Georgia, are you going to perform this year?"

Georgia said, "I don't know yet. Are you?"

Sarah laughed and said, "I'm not sure either."

The final exams were approaching and Sarah was taking more time with her studies than before. This was the big move to the next grade and she wanted to be a seventh grader more than anything.

In *Tai Chi* class, Sifu asked Sarah what was on her mind.

Sarah said, "The big tests are coming up and I am nervous about them."

He told her, "*Tai Chi* philosophy is to let your body do what it was trained for. It knows what to do. Relax, remember to let the energy flow through your body. You have help with the dump sheet, so you must use the keys of training that you have been taught by your instructors and Mrs. Rogers. Have faith in yourself, Sarah, you can pass these tests." Sifu then told her a little secret to think about. "When you enter into *Tai Chi class,* your school work is left at the door. When you leave, you can pick up the school work."

Sarah laughed and thought it was a good idea. She decided to leave her schoolwork in the dressing room. When she changed into her *Tai Chi* clothes, her schoolwork was left hanging in her book bag. This seemed to help Sarah, and the more she worked at hanging up her schoolwork, the easier it was to concentrate in *Tai Chi* class."

Sarah told Mrs. Rogers what Sifu had said and she thought Sifu had a great idea.

"Sarah, when you come through the front door, remember to bring in your schoolwork and leave everything else outside," said Mrs. Rogers

The exam schedule was posted on the classroom bulletin board in each class. Sarah had one test per day for the whole exam week. She thought that was great and couldn't wait to tell her mom and Mrs. Rogers.

Mr. Johnson asked, "Are you going to be in the talent contest again this year?"

Sarah said, "I'm not sure, right now my mind is on the tests, and I haven't practiced anything for the contest."

He smiled and said, "I was hoping you would do the same *Form* that you did last year. My nephew, Ralph, will be enrolling in school. He was a member of *Kung Fu* where he lived." He had told Ralph about Sarah and *Tai Chi*, thinking it would be great to let him know that one of the students from this school was involved in the martial arts.

The contest was a month after the test and she thought she would be able to perform as an intermission act. Sarah said, "Bring Ralph to the Club Center. Sifu will show him around the club and explain the different martial arts that are offered."

The night before the tests, Sarah did *Tai Chi* in her room and it really helped her relax. She studied her notes and practiced the different exercises that Mrs. Rogers had shown her.

The week went by quickly and Sarah felt good about all of her tests. She was a little worried about the math, but thought she would pass. The hard part was waiting until the end of the week to find out. Like last year, she knew she had to put it behind her. Besides, she needed to practice for the show's intermission. She had told Sifu about it and he watched her practice the *Short Form*. Of course, there were always corrections.

Sarah said, "Sifu, even though I worked on *Short Form*, I found there is more to each movement than I thought."

Sifu answered, "Now you understand it is not just learning the *Form*, but learning all the little parts to the form."

Sarah went to the principal and told him she would do *Short Form*, for the show's intermission.

She asked, "Is your nephew here yet?"

Mr. Johnson said, "Ralph will be coming this afternoon."

"Bring Ralph by the Club Center and he will be able to meet Sifu."

Mr. Johnson told Sarah, "That is a great idea and I'll call Sifu and make arrangements to bring Ralph."

After school, Sarah went to Club Center and arrived just as Mr. Johnson and Ralph were getting out of the car. Sarah waved as she walked into the center.

The next day at school Georgia asked, "Have you seen the new boy, Ralph?"

Sarah said, "I saw him at the Club Center, but didn't talk to him."

Georgia said, "He's a hunk and I want to meet him. Can you introduce him to me?"

Sarah laughed, "I don't know him, and so I can't introduce him to you. Besides, he's an eighth grader."

"I wonder why he moved to town now, instead of at the beginning of school?" asked Georgia

Sarah told Georgia what her mother had told her, that he was Mr. Johnson's nephew and would be living with them. His parents had been killed in an auto accident at Christmas, and he had been living with his friend's parents until the semester was over.

Georgia just stood there with her mouth open as a tear slid down her face.

Sarah asked, "Why are you so upset Georgia?"

She didn't answer, but just turned and walked away.

Sarah wondered why Georgia was so upset about what had happened to Ralph and thought she would ask Georgia in science class the next day.

When Sarah arrived home that night, she told her mother about Georgia.

Sarah said, "I'll ask her tomorrow about why she cried."

Sarah's mother said, "We'll talk about it after dinner."

Of course Sarah couldn't eat fast enough to find out what the mystery was about.

After dinner her mother said," Georgia's parents and little sister were all in a car accident and only Georgia lived. It happened about five years ago."

Sarah sat there and at first couldn't say anything, then told her mother, "I guess that's why Georgia acts the way she does." Sarah thought, *I had better try harder to be her friend.*

The next day at school, Sarah didn't mention anything about Ralph or what had happened to Georgia's family. She just sat next to Georgia in science class and tried to act the same way she had always done.

Georgia didn't say much that day either and when class was over, left the room quickly. Sarah tried to hurry after Georgia and as she rushed out of the room she ran smack into Ralph and all of their books went flying.

Ralph helped Sarah up saying, "Gee, I'm sorry, I wasn't looking where I was going."

Sarah laughed and said, "It was my fault too."

Ralph said, "You look familiar. Where have I seen you?"

Sarah said, "We saw each other at Club Center where I take *Tai Chi* class."

The bell rang and Ralph said, "I'll see you at Club Center this afternoon."

As Sarah was leaving school, she met Georgia coming down the hall.

Sarah said, "Hi, guess who I'm going to see at the Club Center?"

Georgia smiled and said, "Let me guess, Ralph."

Sarah laughed and nodded her head, then said, "As soon as I get to know him, I'll introduce you two."

Georgia waved and said, "See you tomorrow Sarah."

The club was full of students that day; it seemed everyone wanted to get some extra practice in. Sarah asked one of the other girls why?

Suzy said, "There is a tournament and the students are just getting in a few more hours of practice before they leave in the morning."

Sarah went into her class and saw Ralph talking to one of the instructors. Sarah said, "Hi, are you going to take *Tai Chi*?"

Ralph said, "No, we were just talking about *Kajukenbo*. They have a class here and I would like to join the group."

The instructor came in and class began for Sarah. She remembered to leave her school thoughts behind and began to work on *Tai Chi*.

The next day in science class, Sarah told Georgia about her meeting with Ralph. She also said how nice he was and knew Georgia would like him. They laughed and went back to work. "Now I can introduce you to him," said Sarah.

Sarah passed her semester exams and was telling Georgia about it when she heard someone call her name. When she turned around, Ralph was standing not too far away from them. Georgia started to leave, but Sarah grabbed her arm.

Ralph came over and said, "Hi, are you going to Club Center today?"

"Yes," and then hurriedly asked, "Have you met my friend, Georgia?"

Ralph said, "Hello," and then offered to carry their books out to the bus. Sarah winked at Georgia and Georgia turned bright red.

At Club Center, Ralph asked what grade Georgia was in and Sarah said, "Sixth."

Ralph said, "Oh, too bad, she is too young for me."

Weeks flew by and it was the dreaded exam study time again. Sarah and Georgia were sitting in science class talking about it, when the teacher came in. He told them that this exam would be on the second half of their book and their notes.

Georgia looked at Sarah and said, "Don't worry, you'll do alright."

The year was coming to a close and the talent show and exams were on everyone's minds. Sarah had been reviewing all of her studies each day and felt she was ready for the exams. Each night before the exam, she would review the work for the next day and then go to bed early.

She met some of her friends outside school and the topic was always the exam that day. The bell rang and Sarah called good luck to her friends and went to her science class. The teacher handed out the exam and the dump sheet.

Sarah read her test over from the first to the last page then began. She remembered if she didn't know the answer to one of the questions, to mark it and then come back to it later. That way she would not panic. She finished and closed her book. When she looked at the clock, there were only a few minutes left in the class.

After class, Georgia asked, "How do you think you did?"

Sarah said, "I think I did alright. How about you?"

Georgia said, "Believe it or not by helping you study and learning some of your study habits, I think I did well too." Georgia said, "I think I am going to sing in the contest."

Sarah said, "Great! I'm going to be part of the intermission." They both laughed.

The day of the talent contest came on a Friday. It was the second to last week before school would be over.

Mr. Johnson said, "Everyone, you must sit quietly and when you've finished your part of the program, bow and walk to the other side of the stage. There you are to sit and wait for the winning announcement."

The talent contest began and everyone was enjoying the show. Sarah's turn came and she went on stage, bowed, and the music and Sarah began as one. Sarah could feel the *Chi* flowing through her body and kept her attention on what she was doing. At the end of her performance, she bowed and everyone clapped. The last person to come on stage was Georgia. She looked beautiful in a soft pink dress. The music began and her voice filled the auditorium with a popular song everyone liked. When she finished, everyone stood up and cheered.

Mr. Johnson announced the third place, then second and finally first. Georgia had won. She came out on stage, and everyone applauded all the winners.

On Monday, everyone was outside school and talking about it being the last full day of school. They would find out if they passed on Wednesday. Wednesday arrived slowly for Sarah. She could hardly wait to see what her grades were.

That morning her mother said, "Eat your breakfast and don't forget to take your *Tai Chi* practice outfit with you today."

Sarah said, "I won't forget and I'll see you after school," as she walked out of the door to the bus.

Everyone sounded excited on the bus as Sarah entered. She sat in the first empty seat she saw and didn't say a word all the way to school. Sarah went to her homeroom and sat down. The students around here were talking about what they would be doing that summer as the teacher walked in.

Jaime and Tristram said, "We're going to go to Oregon and learn how to wind surf."

Cheri, Gina, Kidd, and Maureen, said, "We're going to go to Disneyland in California."

The teacher came into the room and wished them all good luck in the coming school year. She then called each student to her desk. Finally, it was Sarah's turn. It seemed like a long walk up to the front of the room, but she made it and then held out her hand to receive her report card. The teacher smiled and said, "Enjoy your summer, Sarah."

The bell rang for the last time and as the students left the room they said good-bye to the teacher. The hallways filled with laughter, and the buzz of voices, and calls of, "See you next year."

Sarah smiled when she saw Judy and Georgia.

They both said, "Well, are you a seventh grader?"

Sarah said, "YES."

The three girls went out the front door of the school, smiling at each other. Georgia said, "It took a while for me to be friendly. What a waste of time!"

Judy and Sarah said, "Glad we finally got to meet the real you."

As the girls got onto their buses, they called to each other, "See you next year."